Mr Bickle lived alone.

5

Almost.

6

Mr Bickle
and the
GHOST

ReadZone Books Limited

First published in this edition 2015

© in this edition ReadZone Books Limited 2015
© in text Stella Gurney 2007
© in illustrations Silvia Raga 2007

Stella Gurney has asserted her right under the Copyright Designs and Patents Act 1988 to be identified as the author of this work.

Silvia Raga has asserted her right under the Copyright Designs and Patents Act 1988 to be identified as the illustrator of this work.

Every attempt has been made by the Publisher to secure appropriate permissions for material reproduced in this book. If there has been any oversight we will be happy to rectify the situation in future editions or reprints. Written submissions should be made to the Publisher.

British Library Cataloguing in Publication Data (CIP) is available for this title.

Printed in Malta by Melita Press.

ISBN 978 1 78322 472 2

Visit our website: www.readzonebooks.com

Mr Bickle
and the
GHOST

Stella Gurney
and Silvia Raga

He hated having a ghost.

11

It crashed.
"Quiet!"

It sang (terribly).
"Please!"

It went too far.

"Right! Enough!" shouted
Mr Bickle.

The hoover sucked –
the ghost popped.

Peace at last.

Alone again.

Mr Bickle sighed.

He pulled.

"Welcome back," smiled Mr Bickle.

Did you enjoy this book?

Look out for more *Robins* titles –
first stories in only 50 words